Ned Land had swung himself out on to the bowsprit. (Page 12)

The Phoenix Library

Jules Verne

Twenty Thousand Leagues Under the Sea

retold by John Kennett

Blackie : Glasgow and London

Other titles in this series:

Jane Eyre
Charlotte Brontë

Oliver Twist
Charles Dickens

The Count of Monte Cristo
Alexandre Dumas

The Three Musketeers
Alexandre Dumas

Dr. Jekyll and Mr. Hyde
Robert Louis Stevenson

Journey to the Centre of the Earth
Jules Verne

Ben-Hur
Lew Wallace

Copyright © 1958 John Kennett
Illustrations copyright © 1973 Blackie and Son Limited
This edition first published 1973

ISBN 0 216 89689 4

Blackie and Son Limited
Bishopbriggs, Glasgow G64 2NZ
Fitzhardinge Street, London W1H 0DL

Printed in Great Britain by Robert MacLehose & Co. Ltd., Glasgow

JULES VERNE, born in Nantes in 1828, is still one of the world's most popular authors. He practised law for some years before he published his first adventure story in Paris in 1862. From that time he wrote almost at the rate of a novel a year until his death in 1905. It has been said that his books are dreams come true, because he described in them the wonders of modern invention —such as submarines, aeroplanes, and television—long before they became realities.

CONTENTS

CHAPTER ONE

The Monster

*I*T was news that shook **the** world!

In America, the first hint of the danger was in a story printed by the *New York Herald* on 27th June, 1866, under the following headlines:

DAMAGED STEAMSHIP LIMPS HOME

WAS S.S. 'SCOTIA' HOLED BY SEA-MONSTER?

CAPTAIN SPEAKS OF 'GHOSTLY LIGHT'

The report was a strange one. The accident, it seemed, had happened in the dark hours of the morning of 24th June, when the *Scotia*, bound from Liverpool to New York, was three hundred miles off the American coast. Just after four o'clock the officer of the watch had spotted a bright light—" like a giant glow-worm "—on the surface of the sea, and about a quarter of a mile to starboard. The light was oval in shape and burned most brilliantly at the centre. Suddenly it *moved*. It darted straight towards the ship at an unheard of speed and dived beneath it.

The light died out. A slight shock was felt on the hull of the *Scotia*, a little aft of the port-paddle. The ship had been struck, seemingly by something rather sharp and pointed. Even so, there appeared to be no danger of the ship's sinking. She was divided into seven watertight compartments, and could brave any normal leak.

Her captain went down into the hold at once, and found that the sea was pouring into the fifth compartment. The engines were stopped, and a man sent down to find out the extent of the damage. Some minutes later he reported that there was a large hole, two yards across, in the ship's side. Such a leak could not be stopped. The *Scotia* continued her course as fast as she could. She reached New York three days late, and was put in dry dock.

The engineers who examined the damage could scarcely believe their eyes. Two and a half yards below the water-mark was a huge rent, clean-cut in the iron plates, in the shape of a triangle. It could not have been done more neatly by a punch.

The engineers were puzzled; the scientists, when asked for their view, were completely mystified. No one could explain this strange happening. Some of the *Scotia's* crew spoke of seeing a long, dark shape, an enormous thing about three hundred feet long, darting away from the ship after the damage had been done. It was like a great whale, they said, and swore that they had been attacked by some hitherto unknown monster of the deep.

There were, of course, people who laughed at this suggestion. There always are such people.

And then it started. . . . The Terror!

Ship after ship put out to sea—and, as the months passed, it was learned that a great number of them had vanished. First, in the South Atlantic, then in the Indian Ocean, and finally in the South Seas. In something under a year close on two hundred sailing ships and steamships were lost upon the oceans of the world. As the rumours grew and spread, each one was put down as a victim of the " monster ".

There were, however, men who came back. Here and there a lifeboat holding a few survivors was picked up. From time to time a handful of passengers or seamen were saved after their ship had gone down. They all had much the same story to tell. . . .

Their ship had been attacked by some enormous creature of the sea. The thing, whatever it was, had a high turn of speed; at night it shone with an unearthly light; it was larger and more rapid in its movements than a whale.

So the opinion grew that the oceans were now haunted by some terrible monster which had risen from the depths of the seas to strike at ships and their crews.

The Steamship Companies, to begin with, scoffed at the idea and refused to believe that such a monster could exist. Then as the tales of shipwreck and disaster came pouring in they were forced to change their minds. That there really was *something* could not be doubted. Those who did not believe were invited to put their finger on the wound of the *Scotia*.

Public opinion at last forced the governments of the world to take some sort of action. The United States were first in the field. In New York they began preparing an armed frigate of great speed, the *Abraham Lincoln*, to go out and search for the monster along the sea-lanes of the globe; to go out and find the monster—and destroy it.

Then, as always happens, the moment it was decided to pursue the monster, the monster did not appear. For two months no one heard of it. No ship met with it. It seemed as if the creature knew that its life was threatened. So, when the frigate had been armed for the hunt, no one could tell what course it should steer with any hope of finding the monster. A stalemate had been reached.

Then on the 2nd of July, 1867, it was learned that a steamer bound from San Francisco to Shanghai had seen the animal three weeks before in the North Pacific Ocean. The news caused great excitement. The *Abraham Lincoln* was ordered to sail within twenty-four hours.

When the excitement was at its height, there arrived in New York a man whose views on the monster were of immense value. Pierre Arronax, Professor of Natural History in the Museum of Paris, was travelling back to France after spending some months on scientific research in the state of Nebraska.

On the evening of the day of his arrival a leading newspaper came out with this story:

FRENCH SCIENTIST JOINS IN HUNT FOR MONSTER. U.S. GOVERNMENT INVITES ARRONAX TO SAIL AS OBSERVER

Professor Pierre Arronax, the world's greatest authority on undersea life, was this afternoon invited by the Secretary of Marine to sail with the armoured frigate, *Abraham Lincoln,* which is setting out to prove or disprove the existence of the " sea monster " which has for so long been rumoured as responsible for the loss of two hundred ships. The Professor has gladly accepted the invitation. When interviewed by our reporter this afternoon, the famous scientist had this to say concerning the monster:

"The great depths of the ocean are quite unknown to us. Of the beings that live, or can live, twelve or fifteen miles beneath the surface of the waters, we have no idea. The seas have many secrets which they hide from us still. The biggest fish, remember, swim deepest. It is possible that some accident has brought to the upper level of the ocean a creature of huge size that has been hitherto unknown to science. I believe, myself, that it may be a giant narwhale.

"The narwhale often grows to a length of sixty feet. It is armed with a sort of ivory tusk that has the hardness of steel. Some of these sword-like tusks have been found buried in the bodies of whales. Others have been drawn out from the hulls of ships, which they had pierced through and through. There is, indeed, in the Museum of Paris, one of these defensive weapons, two yards and a quarter in length, and fifteen inches round at the thickest part.

"Very well! Suppose this weapon to be six times stronger, and the animal ten times more powerful—and you have a creature very like the 'monster' of which so many sailors have told.

"I believe that such a creature may exist. . . .

"I sail with the *Abraham Lincoln* tomorrow morning. I take with me my assistant Maurice Terray. We both feel that it is our duty to join in the hunt for this disturbing monster, and purge it from the oceans of the world."

So, with these brave words, Professor Arronax made ready to set out on what was to prove one of the greatest adventures of our times. The ocean, with all its secrets, lay before him.

CHAPTER TWO

The Search

"DELIGHTED to have you aboard, Professor. Your cabin is ready for you."

Captain Farragut, commander of the *Abraham Lincoln*, held out his hand as he spoke. He was a man of about forty, spare and hatchet-faced, with bushy eyebrows above a big, strong nose. As he shook hands, his sharp eyes studied with interest the two scientists who had just come aboard his ship. In both cases, he liked what he saw.

Arronax was about the middle height, sturdy and thickset, with reddish hair and a big moustache that did nothing to hide his open and cheerful face. His assistant Terray was a tall, straight young fellow with deep golden hair and wide-set, blue eyes.

The three men shook hands.

" We sail with the tide, gentlemen," said Farragut. " That is, fifteen minutes from now."

The Professor and his assistant remained on deck, watching with interest as the captain

7

ordered the last moorings to be cast loose, and the ship nosed out into the East River. The shore was crowded with spectators. Three cheers burst in a great roar from five hundred thousand throats; half a million handkerchiefs were waved above the heads of the dark mass of people, saluting the frigate all the way until she reached the waters of the Hudson.

Six bells struck as the pilot got into his boat and rejoined the little schooner which was waiting under the frigate's lee.

" Go ahead!" cried Captain Farragut.

The screw beat the waves more rapidly, the frigate skirted the low yellow coast of Long Island; and at eight bells exactly she ran at full steam out on to the dark water of the Atlantic.

In the days that followed it became clear to Professor Arronax that Captain Farragut was a good seaman, worthy of the fine ship he commanded. On the question of the monster there was no doubt in his mind. He believed in it. He was sure that the monster existed, and he had sworn to rid the seas of it. Either Captain Farragut would kill the narwhale, or the narwhale would kill the captain. There was no other way for it.

The crew, as one man, shared this opinion. They asked nothing better than to meet the monster, to harpoon it, hoist it on board—and destroy it. A sum of two thousand dollars had been promised to the first man to sight the creature.

Captain Farragut had seen to it that his ship was well equipped. No whaler had ever been better armed; and, what was more, she had on board Ned Land, the prince of harpooners.

Ned was a Canadian, tall and powerful, whose good looks were in no way spoiled by a nose that was a little flattened as the result of some fight or other. His hair was as black as an Indian's. No other man in the world was his equal in the dangerous trade he followed. It would have to be a cunning whale, indeed, that escaped the stroke of his harpoon.

The frigate drove fast to the south, rounded Cape Horn, and turned her nose towards the Pacific. Excitement mounted high. For weeks the ship scoured the central waters of the world's greatest ocean. Captain Farragut thought it better to stay in deep water, and keep clear of land—as the beast did itself.

The weeks passed, without sight or sign of the monster. The frigate crossed the equator and made for the China Seas. By now, some of the fine enthusiasm of the crew had died down. They were beginning to grow bored.

Then it happened—the thing for which everyone had waited. . . .

The ship was two hundred miles from the coast of Japan. Night had come down; eight bells had just been struck. Large clouds veiled the face of the moon, and the sea rose and fell gently under the vessel's stern.

Professor Arronax was leaning on the rail, a cigar clenched between his teeth. Terray, standing near, was humming softly to himself. Ned Land was perched in the rigging, his keen eyes studying the sea all round.

Suddenly he gave a shout:

" Look out there! the *thing* itself—on our weather beam!"

The Canadian came leaping down from the rigging, and tore towards the bows. The shrill note of the boatswain's whistle twittered along the decks. Men came tumbling to their stations, eyes scanning the dark waters for a sign of the monster.

Captain Farragut gave the order to stop ship.

Professor Arronax raced up to the bridge, his heart beating as if it would break. He could see little in the darkness. No matter how good the Canadian's eyes were, how had the man managed to see—and what had he seen? Could he have been mistaken?

Then came another shout from Ned—and a second later Arronax saw *it* for himself.

Away on the starboard quarter the sea seemed

(H 204)

For hours the Professor and his friends watched the army of fish that escorted the submarine. (Page 34)

to burn in a brilliant oval of light. In the midst of the light there rose a dark, hulking shape.

" It's some sort of phosphorescence on the water," cried one of the ship's officers.

" Nonsense!" snapped Arronax. " Look! It's moving! It's darting towards us!"

A shout of alarm rose from every part of the ship.

" Silence!" roared Farragut. " Up with the helm! Reverse the engines!"

The *Abraham Lincoln* began beating to port in a semi-circle.

" Right the helm, go ahead," cried the captain.

His orders were obeyed. It seemed to Arronax that the frigate began to move away from the burning light.

No, he was mistaken. She tried to sheer off, but the *thing* followed her and came straight for her at a speed that was double her own.

The Professor gasped for breath. Astonishment more than fear held him still and dumb. The *thing* came on, darting through the water at an unheard-of pace. Then it turned away and began to circle the frigate, leaving in its wake electric rings that were like a luminous dust. A minute or two later it drew off, a phosphorescent track marking its course like the clouds of steam an express leaves behind it.

It turned once more and rushed towards the frigate.

There was a shout from Captain Farragut:

" To your gun stations!"

Three cheers greeted this order. The time for the struggle had arrived. Within a matter of seconds the funnels of the frigate were pouring out torrents of black smoke, and the bridge shook under the trembling of the boilers.

Again the *thing* had turned and slowed down. Its track, of a dazzling whiteness, marked its course as it described a long curve.

The frigate drove straight for it. As they drew near, Arronax had a glimpse of Ned Land, who had swung himself out on to the bowsprit. The Canadian stood, one hand clinging to the lines, and the other arm thrown back, with a gleaming harpoon in his fist.

On the frigate drove. Farragut barked an order. His ship came round. Crouching, silent, expectant, the gun crews waited. Every eye on board was trained on that oval of brilliant light that burned on the surface of the dark waters.

Farragut stood with his hands clasped behind his back. He was timing the lurch of his ship and waiting for the guns to bear on his target. His eyes were blazing with excitement. His mouth opened.

" Fire!" he roared.

The starboard guns crashed out in one thunderous roar. The frigate gave a plunge, and for a moment Arronax could see nothing through a cloud of white smoke.

When the smoke billow cleared, he gave a gasp of astonishment. The *thing* was still there, seemingly unharmed.

There was a shout from Ned Land.

" It's coming straight for us! Hard over!"

Arronax saw the Canadian brandishing his terrible harpoon. Then his eyes were fastened on the monster.

It was darting straight for the frigate. Nearer and nearer its light rushed, until it was only a few yards from the ship. Arronax could see the figure of Ned Land silhouetted against its glare. Suddenly his arm straightened, and the harpoon was thrown. There was a loud, ringing noise as if the weapon had struck a hard body. The frigate was turning; men were shouting and bawling; panic reigned on the decks.

The bright light disappeared. There was a fearful shock. The ship heeled right over. Two enormous spouts of water broke over her bridge, rushing like a torrent from stem to stern. Arronax saw a wall of water sweeping down upon him. He clutched at the rail of the bridge, and then the hissing mass of water wrenched him away and hurled him into the sea.

CHAPTER THREE

The Men from the Sea

FOR a moment or two, the Professor was stunned by his fall. The sea took hold of him, and he felt himself drawn down. He was, however, a fair swimmer, and two strong strokes brought him back to the surface.

Even as he gasped for air, and struck out to keep himself afloat, his eyes were searching all round for the frigate. Had anyone seen him washed overboard? Would the captain put out a boat? Might he hope to be saved?

The night was very dark. He caught a glimpse of a black mass drifting away to the east. The ship! Already it seemed a long way off. It was moving away from him. He was lost!

"Help!" he shouted, and struck out for it desperately.

His clothes hindered every move. They seemed glued to his body, weighing him down hopelessly. He was sinking—suffocating.

"Help!"

It was his last cry. His mouth filled with water. He felt himself going down. . . .

His clothes were seized by a strong hand. He felt himself drawn back to the surface of the sea. A voice spoke.

" Hang on to this spar, sir. It's easier than swimming."

The Professor's head cleared. He grabbed at a spar floating on the surface. He saw a face close to his.

" Terray!" he gasped. " So you were thrown into the sea as well!" Terray shook his head.

" No," he said. " I saw you washed overboard and dived in after you." He went on quickly, as the Professor tried to stutter his thanks: " I don't think we can expect any help from the ship. She's drifted off. She must be out of control."

There was a long silence. Both men were thinking. . . .

Had their absence been noticed? How long would it take Captain Farragut to put his steering-gear to rights? Surely, when morning came, he would lower the long-boats and search for the two missing men? It was their only chance. Even so, they would be faced with some eight or nine hours in the water. . . .

" What happened to the—the *thing*?" asked Professor Arronax.

" I don't know," said Terray. " It just

disappeared after it struck the ship. " What d'you think it was, sir?"

" I don't know," Arronax answered. " I'm baffled. I can't even begin to guess. They may know something more about it on board the *Lincoln*. I think we'd better try to steer this spar after the ship. I'm sure they'll search for us as soon as it's light."

The sea, luckily, was very calm. The two of them kicked out, pushing the spar through the water.

A long time passed. In the small hours of the morning, the Professor was seized by cramp. His assistant was forced to hold him up, while the Professor went through thirty minutes of agony.

Then the moon appeared from behind the clouds. The surface of the sea glittered in its rays, and its kindly light put new life into the two men.

Not for long, however. The effort of keeping afloat and pushing the spar began to tell. Slowly, the Professor felt exhaustion creeping through his limbs. He made a despairing effort; half-pulled himself up on to the spar and looked all round. His heart gave a great leap. He could see the ship. She was a long way off—a dark, looming mass.

The Professor tried to shout. It was no use.

His swollen lips could utter no sounds. But Terray began calling out, over and over again:

" Help! Help!"

His shouting ran down into a croak. He fell silent, clinging to the spar and panting hard. The Professor gave a sudden start. Surely, from somewhere, a voice had called across the sea.

" Terray—did you hear?" he gasped.

" Yes!"

Terray gave one last, despairing croak.

This time there was no mistake. A cry had answered his cry. He made a great effort to drag himself up on to the spar. He raised himself half out of the water, then fell back exhausted.

" What did you see?" the Professor gasped.

" 1 saw— " croaked Terray; " I saw—but don't talk—save your strength."

What had he seen? The thought of the monster came into the Professor's head. But that voice? It could not be.

Terray was kicking out, trying to shove the spar through the water. From time to time he raised his head and gave a cry. Each time it was answered by a voice that seemed to draw nearer. The Professor scarcely heard it. He was almost at the end of his strength. His limbs were stiffening. He could hold on no longer. His mouth gaped open, filled with salt water. Cold crept over him. He lifted his head for the last time, and then he sank.

At that very moment a hard body struck him. He clung to it; felt himself being dragged from the water. . . .

He fainted.

There was darkness, and then a sort of thin twilight. He realised that someone was rubbing his hands; that his eyes were open. By the waning light of the moon he saw a face. It was not Terray's, but it was one that he knew immediately.

" Ned Land!" he cried.

" Sure thing," drawled a deep voice. " I'm still in the hunt, Professor."

" Were you thrown into the sea?"

" Nope! I was luckier than you two, I guess. I managed to find a footing on something pretty solid——"

" Solid?"

" Sure—on the back of the monster, to be exact. And I know now why it blunted the point of my harpoon."

" Why, Ned, why?"

" Because, Professor, the beast is made of sheet iron!"

The Professor sat up, startled into life by the Canadian's words. He stared round, then wriggled himself to the top of the thing on which he was lying, half out of the water. He gave a cry of amazement. He kicked the thing. The blow produced a metallic sound. He felt the thing with eager fingers. He knew then that he was touching iron plates, slightly overlaying each other, like the shell which clothes the bodies of certain reptiles.

He studied the thing as best he could in the dim light. Just forward of where he crouched the hull rose to make a low tower that was set in the middle of a platform ringed by an iron rail. A smaller tower was set further aft, behind him. The hull of the thing was long and cigar-shaped; a kind of metal fin rose out of the water behind the after tower.

He gasped. He knew what it was, of course. He sat back on his heels and stared at Ned and Terray.

" A submarine!" he said. " The work of man!"

There could be no doubt of it. The "monster" that had puzzled the scientific world was, in fact, a submarine boat, like a huge fish of steel. As he well knew, it was the first of its kind ever to take to the waters.

Who had built this wonderful machine? What mysteries lay behind it? What kind of beings lived inside it?

His thoughts were rudely interrupted. Just

then a bubbling began at the back of the submarine, and it began to move through the water. The three men had just time to grab for the iron rail before they were swept off. Fortunately, the thing's speed was not great.

" Guess we're all right as long as it keeps like this," Ned cried, " but if it takes a fancy to dive, I wouldn't give two straws for our chances."

There had to be some way of getting in touch with the beings, whoever they were, shut up inside the machine. The Professor began groping all over the platform for a panel or a hatch, but found nothing. The lines of the iron rivets were clear and uniform.

The submarine went on moving through the water. Daybreak appeared. Morning mists surrounded the submarine's hull, but soon cleared off. The Professor began to make his way forward towards the conning tower. . . .

He gave a cry. The vessel was beginning to sink.

" Open up, you water-rats!" roared Ned in a sudden fury, and he began kicking at the iron plates of the tower with his heavy sea-boots.

Almost at once the sinking motion ceased. There was a sound of iron bolts violently pushed aside. A hatch swung open on top of the tower. A man's head and shoulders appeared. He gave an odd cry, and disappeared again. A voice shouted.

As Ned Land took a step towards the open hatch, five strong men appeared, one after the other. Three of them held pistols. One waved his gun and pointed to the open hatch.

The Professor shrugged his shoulders and moved towards it, followed by Ned and Terray. What else could they do?

Arronax lowered himself through the hatch-way until his feet touched an iron staircase. The others followed. For the moment their eyes, dazzled by the outer light, could see nothing. They went down into gloom. Above them the hatch slid shut. At the bottom of the stair, the Professor felt himself seized by strong hands. He was dragged forward. A door opened, he was given a shove. The door slammed shut again. The three were alone—in blackness.

" Say," drawled Ned, " I guess I know now how that feller Jonah felt inside the whale!"

CHAPTER FOUR

Captain Nemo

IN the darkness, Terray laughed.

" They're certainly not overjoyed to see us," he said. " But who are they?"

" Pirates," said Ned. " I'd stake my last dollar on that. Well, I still have my knife tucked in my boot—and I can always see well enough to use *that*. The first one who lays a hand on me——"

" Steady, Ned," said the Professor quietly. " Violence won't help us. Let's try to find out where we are."

He groped about. Five steps took him to an iron wall, made of plates that were bolted together. He turned back and struck against a wooden table, near which stood several stools. The floor was covered with some soft matting, which deadened the noise of their feet. The bare walls showed no trace of door or window. Terray, going the other way round, met the Professor, and they went back to the middle of the cabin.

Half an hour passed while they talked together in low tones. All at once the cabin was flooded with a brilliant light that came from a globe in the roof of the cabin.

The three stood blinking in the sudden glare. A noise of bolts was heard. Ned swung round, knife in hand. The door opened and two men appeared.

Both wore caps made from the fur of the sea otter; both were shod with sea-boots of sealskin; both were dressed in clothes of some elastic material which allowed free movement of the limbs. One was short and broadshouldered, with a thick moustache and very sharp eyes. The other was more striking. He was tall, had a large forehead, straight nose, and black eyes set very wide apart. His skin looked white against the neat dark beard that he wore. This man, clearly the chief on board, examined the three captives without saying a word; then, turning to his companion, spoke to him in an unknown tongue.

The man looked at the Professor, and spoke quickly in the same language. The Professor replied in French that he did not understand. The man shook his head.

The Professor shrugged, and began speaking in English, telling their names and the adventures that had brought the three men so far.

The tall man listened quietly, but nothing in his face showed that he understood a word. The Professor came to the end of his tale.

There was a long silence. All was still as death. Ned Land grew angry.

"Well, what's eating you?" he barked. "What game do you think you're playing with us?"

The tall man looked at him coldly. The short man waved a hand as if to bid Ned hold his tongue. Something seemed to snap inside Ned's head. He gave a roar.

" I guess I know one way to make you talk," he said thickly, and threw himself forward.

Before anyone else could make a move, he had the short man by the throat. The man was choking under the grip of his powerful hand. Terray and the Professor uttered startled exclamations, started forward to drag Ned off, when both were nailed to the spot by hearing these words in English:

" Be quiet, Mr. Land; and you, Professor, be so good as to listen to me."

It was the commander of the vessel who had spoken.

Ned threw his half-suffocated victim from him, and turned. The man he had nearly strangled tottered out on a sign from his master. The Unknown studied the faces before him with narrowed eyes.

" Gentlemen," he said in a calm voice, " I gather that chance has brought before me M. Pierre Arronax, Professor of Natural History; Maurice Terray, his assistant; and Ned Land, harpooner on board the frigate *Abraham Lincoln* of the United States Navy."

The Professor nodded.

" Now that I know you," the Unknown went on, " I have to decide what shall be done with you. You are causing me a great deal of trouble——"

" Quite by accident," said the Professor sharply.

" By accident?" replied the stranger, raising his voice. " Was it by accident that the *Abraham Lincoln* fired at my vessel?"

" Sir," said the Professor quickly, " this submarine vessel of yours has excited the interest of the whole world through its collisions with shipping. No one could explain these accidents. You must understand that, in attacking you, the *Abraham Lincoln* believed itself to be hunting some kind of sea-monster which had to be destroyed at any cost."

A half-smile curled the lips of the Unknown.

" Don't you think that your ship would just as soon have fired at a submarine as a monster?" he asked.

The Professor said nothing.

" You understand then," went on the stranger, " that I have the right to treat you as enemies? I could simply place you upon the deck, where you were found, then sink beneath the waters and forget that you had ever lived."

" That might be the right of a savage," answered the Professor, " but not of a civilized man."

The Unknown smiled grimly.

" I am not what you call a civilized man," he said. His voice took on a harsher note. " I have done with the world of men," he went on. " I no longer obey *your* laws. There was a time when, like you, I was a much-respected scientist. I discovered something—a new form of power, Professor, the power that drives this submarine —and I decided that the world should not have my secret. Do you know why? Because I knew that it would be used for evil purposes—to drive more powerful machines of war, more powerful instruments of destruction. My own nation could have made itself stronger than all others, but I would not give up my secret. And so, Professor Arronax, I was threatened and imprisoned. My wife and children were allowed to starve. They were dead, long before I made my escape. Dead—do you hear? So, Professor Arronax, do not speak to me of laws and civili-

zation. I have suffered too much at the hands
of the world——"

The Unknown's voice had risen. His face
was twisted with hatred. He paused, and took
control of himself. When he went on, his voice
was calm again.

" I have finished with the world of men," he
said. " However, I know something of your
work, Professor. I have read your book on the
depths of the sea. I am ready to spare your life,
and those of your friends, because I think you
may be useful to me. You, I know, will not
regret the time spent on my vessel. I will show
you all the marvels of the sea."

The Professor's eyes glittered with interest.
His weak point was touched.

" You will remain on board my submarine,"
the stranger went on, " and you will be free to
see all that passes here; but you will be here
to *stay*! I cannot permit you to go back to
your own world. You will have seen too
much."

The three captives looked at each other, and
then the Professor turned back to the stranger.

" I don't know who you are," he said, " but
we are grateful to be alive. By what name
should we address you?"

" You may call me Captain Nemo," replied
the commander. " My vessel is the *Nautilus*.

And now, gentlemen, your breakfast is ready. I will lead the way.''

The three men followed Captain Nemo along a passage lighted by electricity. After they had gone a dozen yards a second door opened before them.

They were led into a dining-cabin. High oaken sideboards stood at two ends of the room, and upon their shelves glittered china, porcelain, and glass of great value. The plate on the table sparkled in the rays of light which came from four unpolished globes sunk in the ceiling. There were some first-rate pictures upon the panels of the walls.

Captain Nemo signed for his guests to sit at the table. A steward uncovered the dishes before them. The three looked uncertainly at the food on the dishes. Captain Nemo smiled.

'' These dishes are quite unknown to you,'' he said, '' but you may eat without fear. They all come from the ocean, and they are all wholesome and nourishing. I have given up the food of the earth, and I am never ill now. That dish which looks like meat, Professor, is fillet of turtle. Here are some dolphins' livers. The cream is milk from the sperm whale, the sugar is taken from a seaweed of the North Sea. Lastly, let me beg you to try the fruit—preserves made of sea anemones.''

The three men ate, nervously at first, and then with good appetite. When the meal was over Captain Nemo rose.

" Gentlemen," he said, " if you wish to go over the *Nautilus*, I am at your service."

They rose and followed him. A double-door at the back of the dining-cabin opened, and they entered another large cabin.

It was a library. High cabinets supported upon their wide shelves a great number of books. Bright light flooded everywhere.

From the library they passed into a big saloon, where a soft, clear light fell on marvels that made the Professor exclaim aloud.

Under elegant glass cases, fixed by copper rivets, were classed and labelled many hundreds of plants and creatures taken from the sea. There were shells and specimens which the Professor had never seen before. Captain Nemo smiled at his obvious delight.

" I collected them all with my own hand," he said. " There is not a sea on the face of the globe that I have not explored for its wonders."

" Say, Captain," drawled Ned Land, " there's an awful lot of instruments that mean nothing to a simple fellow like me."

He waved a hand at a large number of instruments hanging from the walls of the cabin, and screwed into the top of a long table.

" They tell me all I need to know concerning
the speed, direction, and depth of my vessel.
Some, like the barometer and compass, are
already known to you. Others are of my own
invention. I have them always under my eyes.
This planisphere on the table will give you our
exact position at a glance. Our course is
marked off every two hours throughout the day
and night."

The tour went on. The four men passed from
cabin to cabin—through kitchens, bathrooms,
and into an engine-room about sixty feet long.
The engine itself was shrouded by a screen of
some dull metal that looked like lead.

" It is not safe for you to go behind that
screen," the Captain told them. " I have
harnessed a new form of power, known to no
other living man. It can give me an underwater
speed of fifty miles an hour. It also gives me
light and heat, at a ridiculously small cost. The
pumps of the *Nautilus* have an enormous power,
as you must have seen when their jets burst
upon your ship."

" The light!" exclaimed Ned Land suddenly.
" What causes the light that we saw from the
Lincoln's decks?"

" Electric reflectors that light up the sea in
front of my helmsman," he said. " Searchlights, if you like to call them that."

" Captain," said Terray, shaking his head in wonder, " your *Nautilus* is, without doubt, the finest vessel the world has seen."

Captain Nemo looked pleased.

" We, on board, need fear no dangers," he said. " Storms and gales leave us untouched; there is no rigging to attend to; no sails for the wind to carry away; no boilers to burst; no fire to fear, for the vessel is made of iron; no collision to fear, for it alone swims in deep water."

" But how could you build it in secret?" asked Terray.

" Each part was ordered from different countries. I set up my workshops upon a lonely desert island. There my workmen—whom I had carefully chosen, instructed and educated—built my *Nautilus*. When our work was finished, fire destroyed all traces upon our island. No one would know that we had ever been there."

" And the cost?" asked the Professor.

Captain Nemo shrugged.

" It ran into several millions," he said.

Arronax raised an eyebrow.

" You are rich?" he asked.

" I hardly missed the sum that was spent," said Captain Nemo simply.

Three men stared at him. Who, they wondered, was this unknown who called himself Captain Nemo—*nemo*, the Latin for 'no-body'. Why had he built the *Nautilus*? What mystery surrounded his life? What would happen next. . . .

Only the future could tell them that.

CHAPTER FIVE

The Submarine Forest

EARLY the next day, Professor Arronax and his friends were permitted to go out on to the upper platform of the *Nautilus*, which had surfaced so that Captain Nemo might take a fix of the sun.

The submarine, they saw, was more than two hundred feet long. It was shaped like a cigar, with the platform set amidships. At the base of the after tower was bolted a boat, that could be slid into a cavity specially made for it. Ned Land took a great deal of interest in this boat. . . .

The sea was beautiful, the sky pure. The *Nautilus* hardly seemed to feel the movements of the ocean. There was nothing in sight.

Captain Nemo fixed his position.

" Two o'clock, gentlemen," he said. " When you are ready——"

A little reluctantly, they cast a last look upon the sea and went down to the saloon. There they were left alone.

The Professor bent over the planisphere and placed his finger on the little cross that marked the present position of the submarine, some thirty or forty miles off the coast of Japan.

"Where are we?" asked Ned Land. "We can see nothing in this iron prison."

He had no sooner spoken than the lights went out. A sliding noise was heard. Two long panels on either side of the saloon slid back, and light broke through two oblong openings, sealed by material that looked like glass. The three men stared in wonder through these observation-ports. The sea was clearly visible for a mile all round the *Nautilus*, and, in the electric brightness produced by the submarine, it was as if they were travelling through a vast pool of liquid light.

It was like moving through the waters of an immense aquarium. For hours the Professor and his friends watched the army of fish that escorted the submarine. There were fish of every size and shape and colour, from the white-tailed goby with violet spots on its back, to spider lampreys which were six feet long and had huge mouths bristling with teeth.

The Professor, of course, was in ecstasies to see, alive and at liberty, all the fish of the seas of China and Japan. He began sketching and making notes. . . .

Suddenly the lights came on once more. The iron panels closed over the ports, and that strange sea-world disappeared. The rest of the day passed without another visit from Captain Nemo.

He was at breakfast, however, when the three appeared next morning. He seemed in good humour.

" Gentlemen," he said, " you have seen something of the world over which I rule. Now I should like you to know more about it. I am inviting you to join me in a hunting-party."

The three stared at him, puzzled.

" Then you are planning to go ashore?" the Professor asked.

Captain Nemo smiled.

" No," he said. " I mean to hunt at the bottom of the sea. There are forests that grow there as well as on land—and the shooting is just as good. I will supply you with diving-suits."

" And the guns?" asked Ned.

" Air-guns of my own design," answered Captain Nemo. " I use air under great pressure, supplied to me by the pumps of the *Nautilus*. The guns fire little cartridges of glass, which are covered with a case of steel, and weighted with a pellet of lead. Electricity is forced into each pellet to a very high tension. With the slightest shock they are discharged, and the animal, however strong it may be, falls dead. But eat your meal, gentlemen, and then you shall see for yourselves.''

As soon as breakfast was over, Captain Nemo led the three men aft, and took them into a small chamber behind the engine-room. A dozen or so diving-suits hung from its walls.

Two of the crew were called to help the Professor and his friends into their underwater suits. These were of india-rubber without seams. The trousers were finished off with thick boots, weighted by heavy leaden soles, and the sleeves ended in gloves. Air cylinders were fixed on to their backs by straps. The upper part of the suit ended in a copper collar, upon which was screwed the metal helmet. Three holes, protected by thick glass, allowed the wearer to see in all directions simply by turning his head. Set in the casing of the helmet, above the glass, was a small electric lantern.

As soon as the Professor's helmet had been screwed down, and the breathing apparatus had been tested, one of the *Nautilus* men handed him a simple gun. The butt end, which was large, was made of steel and hollow in the centre. This served as a reservoir for the compressed air, which the trigger allowed to escape into the

metal tube of the barrel. Each gun fired twenty
shots. As soon as one shot was fired, another one
was ready.

The Professor felt glued to the deck by his
leaden soles. He tried to walk and couldn't.
It was impossible for him to take a step. The
two *Nautilus* men, however, pushed him into a
little room next door, along with his companions. He heard a watertight door close upon
him, and was wrapped in thick darkness.

He heard a loud hissing sound. As the diving-
chamber filled with water, he felt the cold
mount from his feet to his chest. A second door
then opened in the outer wall of the *Nautilus*.
He saw a faint light. Captain Nemo took hold
of his arm and urged him forward. It was no
longer difficult to move. A few seconds later
and his feet were set on the bottom of the sea.

Above him hovered the long, sleek shape of
the submarine, its searchlights gleaming through
the water. He could see clearly for a con-
siderable distance. He no longer felt the weight
of his clothing, or his thick helmet, or the leaden
shoes.

Captain Nemo moved away from the submarine. The others followed some steps
behind. Above them now was the calm surface
of the sea. They were walking on fine sand, and
at a depth of thirty feet the Professor found that

he could see as well as if he was in broad
daylight.

Behind them the hull of the *Nautilus* slowly
disappeared, but its searchlights, when darkness
settled upon the waters, would help to guide
them back.

Captain Nemo walked on as if he knew every
inch of the way. Soon the sand gave way to a
plain of seaweed, among which stood many
rocks, with around them brilliant gardens of
flowers in yellow and green, orange, violet, and
blue.

They went on for almost two hours, when
the ground took on a downward slope, and they
began to move in a sort of reddish twilight.
Then Captain Nemo stopped and pointed ahead
to a dark, looming mass.

" It's the underwater forest," the Professor
thought—and was not mistaken.

The forest was made up of large tree-plants,
whose branches all stretched up towards the
surface of the ocean. Fishes of all shapes and
sizes swam among the trees like birds, and here
and there were bushes of living flowers.

Captain Nemo led the way among the trees
for yet another hour. He then gave a signal to
halt, and the four men stretched themselves
under a tree whose branches stood up like
arrows.

The Professor found that he was terribly hungry, but since eating was out of the question, he lay back and closed his eyes—and fell into a doze. When he awoke, Captain Nemo had already risen. The Professor was on the point of rising, when he saw something that made him freeze on the spot.

Only a few steps off, a monstrous sea-spider, about thirty-eight inches high, was watching him with squinting eyes, making ready to spring. Even though his diving-suit was thick enough to defend him from the bite of the hideous creature, he shuddered with horror at the sight. A second later a blow from the butt of Captain Nemo's gun smashed down upon the creature, and the Professor saw its horrible claws writhing in agony. It occurred to him that other animals, even more to be feared, might haunt these shadowy depths.

Captain Nemo stepped forward. Above them the sun seemed to be blinking. As they went on the darkness deepened. The Professor was groping his way, when he saw a brilliant light ahead. Captain Nemo had switched on his lantern, and the others did the same. The sea now was lit up for a circle of thirty-six yards all round.

Still Captain Nemo plunged on into the dark depths of the forest. Then, suddenly, he

shouldered his gun and fired. There was a slight
hissing noise, and the Professor saw a creature
fall through the water some yards ahead. It was
a magnificent sea-otter, chestnut-brown above
and silvery underneath, with webbed feet and
sharp nails, and a tufted tail.

Captain Nemo threw the beast over his
shoulder, and turned back the way he had come.
On the four marched, till they were once more
in shallow water. The Professor found that he
was tiring rapidly. He was beginning to feel
that he could not walk another pace when he
saw a glimmer of light, which, for half a mile,
broke the darkness of the waters. It was the
searchlight of the *Nautilus*.

The Professor was lagging some steps behind,
when he saw Captain Nemo turn and come
hurrying back. He switched off his lantern and
signed for the others to do the same. With his
strong hand he forced the Professor to the
ground, waved to the others, and lay down
himself.

The Professor was lying under the shelter of a
great bush of weed. Puzzled by Nemo's action,
he raised his head and stared all round. He saw
two great shapes go blustering by.

The blood froze in his veins. They were huge
sharks with enormous tails, silver bellies, and
great razor-edged jaws.

The creatures, luckily, passed the little party without seeing them, just brushing them with their brownish fins.

Inside an hour, guided by the searchlight, they had reached the *Nautilus*. The outside door had been left open, and Captain Nemo closed it as soon as they had entered the first chamber. He then pressed a knob. The Professor felt the water sinking from around him, and in a few minutes the diving-chamber was empty. The inside door was opened—and they were safely back inside the submarine.

CHAPTER SIX

The Pearl Diver

DAYS and weeks passed while the *Nautilus* steered a steady course across the Sea of Japan and into the Indian Ocean. By the 28th of January, 1868, the submarine had travelled twelve thousand miles with the Professor and his friends.

When the *Nautilus* surfaced at noon of that day, there was land in sight about eight miles to the west. The first thing the Professor noticed was a range of mountains lifting their craggy heads above the horizon.

" The island of Ceylon," said Captain Nemo, " noted for its pearl-fisheries. Would you like to visit one of them, Professor?"

" I should indeed."

" Well, that's easily arranged. By the way, you are not afraid of sharks?"

" Sharks!" exclaimed the Professor.

The question seemed a hard one to answer. He thought about it.

" I must admit, Captain," he added, " that I

am not a great lover of that kind of fish.''

'' *We* are used to them,'' replied Captain
Nemo, '' and in time you will be, too. However, we shall be armed, and on our way we may
be able to hunt a shark or two. It is interesting.
But you shall see for yourself, early tomorrow
morning. . . .''

Next morning at four o'clock, the Professor
was awakened by a steward. He rose, dressed,
and went into the saloon. Captain Nemo was
waiting for him.

'' Are you ready to start?'' he asked.

'' Yes.''

'' Come, then. Your friends are on the
platform.''

'' Shan't we wear our diving-suits?'' the Professor asked.

'' Not yet. I have not brought the *Nautilus*
too close in. The boat will carry us as far as we
want to go. The diving-gear has been loaded
into it.''

The boat, as the Professor knew, was attached
to the upper part of the hull. It was decked over
when the submarine dived.

He followed Captain Nemo up to the platform. Ned and Terray were already there, delighted at the idea of the outing before them.
Five sailors from the *Nautilus* were in the boat
alongside, resting on their oars.

4

It was not yet light. Layers of cloud covered the sky, allowing only a few stars to be seen.

The boat moved in towards the coast. The light grew until suddenly it was bright day. The sun pierced the curtain of cloud and rose rapidly. Land could be seen quite clearly, about five miles off, with a few trees scattered here and there.

Captain Nemo gave a sign. The anchor was dropped, but the chain scarcely ran, for the water was little more than a few feet deep.

Helped by the sailors, Captain Nemo and the others began to put on their heavy diving-suits. Soon they were enveloped to the throat in india-rubber clothing. Before putting his head into the copper helmet, the Professor noticed that it was not fitted with a lamp.

" We shan't be going deep enough to need one," Captain Nemo told him. " Besides, it would not be a good thing in these waters— might attract the sharks."

The Professor gulped.

" Where are our guns?" he asked.

" Guns!" exclaimed Nemo. " What for? Here is a strong dagger. Put it in your belt. Now, let's get started."

A minute later the Professor's helmet was screwed down. The air supply was switched on, and the four were ready to start. They went

over the side and landed, one after the other,
upon even sand. Captain Nemo made a sign with
his hand, and they followed him down a gentle
slope into deeper water.

Over their feet rose shoals of fish of every
shape and colour. The sand gave way to a sort of
open plain strewn with boulders, where there
swam rock-fish three and a half feet long.

An hour later they found themselves facing
the oyster-banks on which the oyster pearls are
reproduced in millions.

Captain Nemo led the others on by paths
known only to himself, among high rocks
where waited huge crabs and lobsters, which
perched upon their claws and watched the
men go by with fixed eyes

Soon there opened before them a large cave,
dug in a heap of rocks. At first sight it looked
very dark, but when Captain Nemo entered and
the others followed, they found that their eyes
soon grew used to the green and watery light.
A slope took them down into a large, round pit.
There Captain Nemo stopped and pointed with
his hand. The Professor moved forward, stared
hard and gasped.

He was looking at a huge oyster, about two
and a half yards across, stretched across a big
rock with a flat top.

Captain Nemo seemed to have known it was

there. Its shells were a little open. The Captain
put his dagger between them to stop them
snapping shut, prised them apart, and stood
aside. The Professor found himself looking at a
loose pearl, nearly the size of a coconut. It
must have been of immense value. The Professor stretched out his hand to seize it, but the
Captain stopped him, quickly withdrew his
dagger, and let the two shells close. The Professor then thought he understood. In leaving
this pearl, Captain Nemo was allowing it to
grow slowly. As it was, it must have been worth
tens of thousands of pounds.

Captain Nemo moved back out of the cave,
and they travelled on for another ten minutes.
Suddenly Nemo stopped. He sank down and
made a sign for the others to do the same. He
pointed, and shook his head.

About five yards from him, the Professor saw
a shadow appear and sink down to the sea-bed.
It was a man, a living man, an Indian, a fisherman
diving for pearls. The Professor could see the
bottom of his boat, anchored and still on the
surface of the sea. The man dived and went up
again several times. He held a stone between
his feet, to bring him down more rapidly, and a
rope fastened the stone to his boat. As soon as
he reached the bottom, he went on his knees
and began filling his bag with oysters. Then he

went up, emptied it, pulled up his stone, and began the operation once more.

He did not see the men from the *Nautilus*, for they were hidden in the shadow of the rock.

They stayed still and watched him go up and down for about half an hour. Then, as he crouched on the sea-bed, the Professor saw the man look up and make a movement of sheer terror. He made a spring to return to the surface of the sea.

A second later the Professor understood his dread. A gigantic shadow had flickered in the water above the unlucky man's head. It was a shark—making for him with eyes on fire and jaws wide open.

It shot straight at the diver. The man threw himself on one side to avoid the shark's fins; but not its tail, which struck his chest and stretched him flat on the bed of the sea.

The shark turned on its back, and moved in to cut the diver in two.

The Professor, filled with horror, could make no move. He saw Captain Nemo rise, dagger in hand, and leap towards the monster. It turned over and shot straight for him.

CHAPTER SEVEN

The Arabian Tunnel

CAPTAIN Nemo halted. He fell into a crouch and waited for the shark to come to him. As it dived for him, he threw himself to one side, and buried his dagger deep into its side.

Blood gushed in torrents from the wounded shark. The sea was dyed red and, for a second or two, the Professor could see nothing more. Nothing more until the moment when he made out Captain Nemo hanging on to one of the creature's fins, and dealing blow after blow at his enemy, yet still unable to kill it.

The shark's struggles whipped up the water with such fury that the rocking almost upset the Professor. He wanted to go to the Captain's assistance, but, nailed to the spot with horror, he could not stir.

All at once the Captain fell to the sea-bed, upset by the weight thrown upon him. The shark's jaws opened wide. It closed in. All seemed over with Captain Nemo; but, quick as thought, Ned Land rushed towards the shark.

Above his head he was swinging a harpoon that he had brought with him instead of a dagger. He buried its sharp point in the creature's flesh.

The waves rocked under the shark's movements. Terray started forward, and was thrown over almost at once. But Ned Land had not missed his aim. The shark was struck to the heart. Even now, its struggles were growing weaker.

Ned Land went to Captain Nemo's side. The Captain rose, unhurt, moved over to the Indian, lifted the man in his arms, and, with a sharp blow of his heel, rose to the surface.

The others followed. Together they tipped the diver into his boat, and climbed in after him.

The man sprawled in the bottom of the boat. Captain Nemo bent over him and began working to bring him back to life. It was a hopeless task, the Professor thought. The underwater struggle had lasted little more than a minute, but the blow from the shark's tail might have been the man's death-blow.

Then, incredibly, the diver opened his eyes. His face took on a look of terror when he saw the four great copper heads leaning over him. Captain Nemo straightened up, took from the pocket of his suit a bag of pearls, and placed them in the man's hand.

The diver gaped, trembling in every limb.

A moment later and the four had dropped once more down to the bed of the sea. Led by Captain Nemo, they trudged back the way they had come. In just over half an hour they reached the anchor which held the boat from the *Nautilus*.

Once on board, they made haste to get rid of their heavy helmets. Captain Nemo's first words were to the Canadian.

" Thank you, Mr. Land," he said; and that was all.

The boat flew over the waves. Minutes later, they met with the shark's dead body floating on the sea. It was more than twenty-five feet long, and its enormous mouth stretched over a third of its body. There were six rows of teeth in the upper jaw.

Even while the men were studying it, a dozen more of the creatures appeared round the boat, threw themselves upon the dead body, and fought with one another for the pieces.

At half-past eight the little party were once more on board the *Nautilus*. She had dived before they breakfasted, and drove on beneath the waves.

Again the days passed. For the Professor and Terray, they were days of wonder and delight. They were scientists, first and foremost, and this voyage beneath the waters gave them an unrivalled opportunity to study the creatures of the ocean. For Ned Land, however, things were very different. He was growing moody and restless, and toying with ideas of escape.

The *Nautilus* crossed the Indian Ocean and entered the Red Sea. The Professor was puzzled by this. Since Captain Nemo could not openly use the Suez Canal, it seemed certain that sooner or later he would have to turn back upon his tracks.

Still the submarine steered a course to the north. When she surfaced one morning, Captain Nemo mounted to the platform, where the Professor was taking the air.

" Well, does the Red Sea please you?" Nemo asked. " Have you seen enough of its wonders? Unfortunately, I cannot take you through the Suez Canal, but tomorrow we shall be in the Mediterranean."

The Professor stared at him in astonishment.

" The Mediterranean!" he exclaimed. " What fearful speed will have to be put on the *Nautilus* if she is to be in the Mediterranean tomorrow—having doubled the Cape of Good Hope and sailed all the way round Africa?"

Captain Nemo smiled.

" Who told you that she would make the round of Africa?" he asked.

" Well, unless she sails on dry land, or passes above it——"

" Or beneath it, Professor."

" Beneath it?"

" Certainly," said Nemo quietly. " A long time ago Nature made a tunnel under the tongue of land that separates us from the Mediterranean. I call it the Arabian Tunnel. It will take us beneath Suez and under Port Said——"

" Can this be true?" the Professor gasped. " How did you discover this tunnel?"

" I noticed," said Nemo, " that in the Red Sea and in the Mediterranean there lived certain fishes that are exactly the same. I therefore asked myself if it was possible that there could be an unknown passage between the two seas. I caught a large number of fishes near Suez, passed copper rings through their tails, and threw them back into the sea. Some months later, off the coast of Syria, I caught some of my fish marked with the rings. I knew then that I was right: the tunnel was there, waiting to be found. I discovered it, ventured into it—and before long you, too, sir, will have passed through my Arabian Tunnel!"

The *Nautilus* that evening was in the Gulf of Suez. She surfaced a little after nine. The Professor went up to the platform, where he was joined by Captain Nemo.

Through the dusk they could see a light shining.

" The floating light of Suez," said Captain Nemo. " It won't be long before we gain the entrance of the Tunnel."

" The entrance cannot be easy."

" It isn't. For that reason I shall take the helm myself. Now, if you will go down, Professor, we are going to dive. We shall not return to the surface until we are in the Mediterranean."

The Professor went down to the saloon and sat beside an observation-port. The submarine dived. Outside, the sea appeared vividly lit up. The Professor looked in silence at the high straight wall they were running by at that moment, the base of a high, sandy coast. They followed it for something over an hour, keeping only a few yards off.

At a quarter past ten, a large gallery, black and deep, opened before them. The *Nautilus* went boldly into it. A strange roaring was heard round its sides, made by the waters of the Red Sea rushing violently towards the Mediterranean. The submarine went with the torrent, rapid as an arrow, even though the screw had been thrown over into reverse.

On the walls of the narrow passage, the Professor could see nothing but brilliant rays, straight furrows of fire, traced by their great speed under the brilliant electric light. His heart beat fast.

At thirty-five minutes past ten, Captain Nemo appeared in the doorway of the saloon.

" The Mediterranean!" he said.

In less than twenty minutes the torrent had carried the *Nautilus* from one sea to the other.

CHAPTER EIGHT

The Ice-fields

THE submarine surfaced soon after dawn. The Professor hastened to the platform. There was no land in sight. A few minutes later he was joined by Ned and Terray.

The Canadian looked all round at the quiet sea, then drew close to the Professor's side.

" So we're in the Mediterranean," he said. " Great! That's a swell piece of luck! We're close to Europe, Professor. Now's the time to make our getaway."

The Professor frowned. In his heart, at that moment, he had no wish to leave the submarine. Thanks to Captain Nemo and the *Nautilus*, he was re-writing his book on underwater life. Would he ever again have the chance to see at first hand the wonders of the ocean? Could he bring himself to leave the *Nautilus* before his work was done?

" Ned," he said slowly, " I'm not sorry to have made this journey under the seas——"

" Maybe not," said Ned, " but where's it all going to end?"

" I don't know. On the other hand, I agree with you that it's only good sense to try and make our escape at the first reasonable opportunity."

" There'll never be a better chance than we shall have during these next few days," said Ned eagerly. " We can wait for a dark night, when we're not too far from a coast. I've been having a look at the Captain's boat. We can get away in that."

The Professor nodded, a little reluctantly.

" All right," he agreed. " We'll do it if the chance occurs. Don't forget that one hitch could ruin us. Now that we're so close to Europe, Captain Nemo will be expecting us to try something of the sort. He'll be on his guard."

" We'll see," said Ned, a determined look on his face. " I'm beginning to think that Captain Nemo's just plumb crazy. . . ."

The days passed and the chance to escape did not come. The *Nautilus* steered the length of the Mediterranean beneath the waves, as if Captain Nemo felt himself cramped between the close shores of Africa and Europe. The submarine passed through the Straits of Gibraltar and put out into the Atlantic. Ned Land, to his great disgust, was forced to give up his idea of flight—for the moment. . . .

Where were they going now? They had no idea.

The *Nautilus* went far out into the Atlantic and turned south, making a speed of twenty miles an hour, at a depth of about fifty fathoms.

The Professor and Terray spent most of their time studying the fish of these waters through the panels in the side of the submarine.

They moved at last into an area where the sea-bed became rocky and mountainous. Finally, their way seemed blocked by a high wall, whose summit seemed to rise above the level of the ocean. The *Nautilus* moved in close beside the wall and rose to the surface.

A minute or two later there was a trampling sound on deck.

" I can't believe it," said Terray. " Captain Nemo has come in to the land. Let's see where we are."

They went up to the platform. The Professor was the first to step out. He gasped in utter astonishment.

The submarine's scarchlights only partly lit up the great cavern in which she floated, near a mountain which formed a sort of quay. All around was a huge lake, shut in by a circle of walls. High above, the walls leaned into a vaulted roof. There was a hole in the roof through which there came a gleam of daylight.

Captain Nemo approached.

" Where are we?" the Professor asked.

" Underground," said Nemo. " We are in the heart of a dead volcano, whose crater has been invaded by the sea. The *Nautilus* entered this lagoon by a natural canal, which opens about thirty feet under the surface of the sea. The volcano belongs to an island. To other ships it is a dead and useless rock—but for the *Nautilus* it is a perfect harbour."

" A harbour, Captain?" said Terray. " The *Nautilus* wants no harbour, surely."

" Perhaps not—but it wants fuel to make it move; and this is where I get my fuel, both sodium and coal. On this spot the sea covers great forests, which have been crushed into coal. However, my need this time is for sodium, of which I have here a reserve supply. We shall be loading for one day only. The *Nautilus* does not rest long in one spot. We sail again tonight."

For the rest of that day the crew of the submarine were busy loading sodium, and at nightfall the *Nautilus* left its port and steered out once more into the ocean. The course was due south.

On and on the vessel drove as day followed day. The Professor had an idea that when on a

Long metal rods were sunk in the side walls. (Page 73)

level with Cape Horn Captain Nemo would turn west and make for the Pacific once more. He did nothing of the kind, however, but continued on his way to the far south.

Where was he going? The Professor began to think that perhaps Ned Land was right—that Captain Nemo was " just plumb crazy ".

The *Nautilus* drove well inside the Antarctic polar circle. Again and again, the submarine was surrounded by ice on every side. Always, however, Captain Nemo found an opening, through which he boldly slipped, knowing that it would close again behind him. Guided by his skilful hand the *Nautilus* passed through the ice in a manner that made the Professor gasp— slipping by huge icebergs and great floating packs of ice, the nose always pointed south.

It was very cold on deck, but everyone now wore the furs of seal or sea-bear. Inside the sub-marine, the electrical heating held back the bitter cold.

Sometimes the ice took on the most sur-prising shapes. In places great blocks of it rose up, like an oriental town, with mosques and minarets gleaming in a pallid sunshine. Some-times the whole, white world of it was blotted out by hurricanes of driving snow, or lost in thick, grey fog. Often, when he could see no way through, the Professor thought that they were prisoners of the ice, but always Captain Nemo found a new pass. He was never mistaken when he saw the thin threads of blue water trickling among the pack-ice, and the Professor had no doubt that he had voyaged in these cold and bitter seas before.

Then there came a morning when the ice-field solidly blocked their road in one vast stretch of ice cemented by the cold.

Even this could not stop Captain Nemo. He drove the submarine at it with frightful violence. The *Nautilus* cut into the brittle mass like a wedge and split it with loud cracklings. The ice, thrown high into the air, fell like hail all round.

Slowly but surely, the submarine hacked out a path for itself; sometimes it lodged on the ice-field, crushing it with its weight; and sometimes it was buried beneath it, dividing it by a simple pitching movement that made large cracks in the ice.

Strong and biting winds blew all the time this was going on. The snow lay on deck in such hard heaps that the crew had to break it with pickaxes. The temperature was at five degrees below zero and every outward part of the *Nautilus* was thickly coated with ice.

Then there came a morning when it was clear that even Captain Nemo could not drive his vessel further south. The way was blocked solid not by the ice-field but by mountainous bergs, soldered together by the bitter cold. There was not even a glimpse of the sea ahead. Everything was still and frozen.

On deck, Captain Nemo studied the desolate scene all round. The Professor was at his side.

" Captain," said the Professor, " I think that we are caught."

" Do you really think so?" asked Nemo. " My dear sir, I tell you that the *Nautilus* can not only free itself, but can also go far to the south of this point."

The Professor stared.

" Farther to the south?" he asked.

" Yes. It shall go to the pole."

In that moment, the Professor made up his mind that Captain Nemo *was* indeed a madman.

" I can well believe you, Captain," he said ironically. " Let us go ahead! Let us smash a way through! Let us blow up these icebergs! And if we can't do that, let us give the *Nautilus* wings to fly over them!"

" No, not that," said Nemo quietly, " but *under* them. The surface may be frozen, but the lower depths are not. For one foot of iceberg above the sea there are three below it. If these ice mountains are not more than three hundred feet above the surface, then they are not more than nine hundred beneath. And what are nine hundred feet to the *Nautilus*?"

The Professor was now staring at him with eager eyes, fired by the thought of sailing *beneath* the South Pole.

" The only difficulty," continued Captain Nemo, " is that of remaining several days without renewing the air-supply. Once we have set out, we shall not be able to surface until we have found open sea once more."

" Is that all?" asked the Professor. " Surely the *Nautilus* has vast reservoirs of air? They can supply us with all the oxygen we need."

" You are a man after my own heart," said Captain Nemo. " We'll get ready to start at once."

All that afternoon the pumps of the submarine were working air into the reservoirs and storing it at high pressure. At four o'clock Captain Nemo announced that the submarine was ready to submerge.

The weather, for once, was clear. About ten men of the crew began breaking the ice around the vessel with pickaxes. It was not hard to do, for the fresh ice that had built up along the sides was still very thin.

An hour later all was ready. Professor Arronax threw one last look at the icy landscape, then turned and went down to the saloon.

The great, metal hatches were screwed down. The long, metal hull of the submarine sank beneath the water—and the ice—her commander now intent on taking her beneath the South Pole.

CHAPTER NINE

Trapped

THE Professor sat in the saloon, gazing through an observation-port. They were floating, at a depth of nine hundred feet, beneath the bottom of a great iceberg. Still the *Nautilus* sank lower, nosing down into the depths to make sure of a free passage. In forty hours, if all went well, she would be underneath the pole.

The sea all round was brilliantly lit by her searchlights, but it was deserted. Fish did not live in these imprisoned, icy waters.

The submarine's pace was rapid. It could be felt in the quivering of the long steel body. For a large part of the previous night the Professor and his friends had remained in the saloon, held there by the novelty of their situation. About three in the morning, however, they had all taken some sleep, then come back to their posts in the saloon. They had seen nothing of Captain Nemo, and supposed him to be at the helm.

The hours passed; the submarine drove on.

Once there came a shock, that told them that the *Nautilus* had struck the bottom of an iceberg at a depth of two thousand feet. This meant that there must be three thousand feet of ice above, one thousand being above the water-mark.

Several times that day they felt these little shocks, and each time it happened Captain Nemo took his vessel deeper still until he found a clear road.

Night came once more. Breathing was just a little hard, but Captain Nemo had not yet made any demands upon his reserve supply of oxygen.

It was not easy to sleep that night, the Professor found. When he did at last drop off, he was haunted by terrible dreams in which he found himself trapped in the *Nautilus* hundreds of feet below the ice-fields.

The next day dragged itself along. At length, just after four in the afternoon, the door of the saloon opened and Captain Nemo appeared.

" Gentlemen," he said, " we are now under the pole. We have achieved something that no human being has done before. We may not linger, however, but steer to the north as fast as we are able."

By then they were drawing upon their reserve supply of air.

The *Nautilus* sped to the north all through that day and into the night. When the Professor settled himself to sleep it was floating under the body of an immense iceberg.

He was awakened by a violent shock. He sat up in bed and listened in the darkness, and then the submarine tilted hard over and he was thrown into the middle of the room.

He picked himself up, feeling a little shaky, and groped his way along the walls of his cabin, through the door, and down to the saloon, where the lights were still burning. Most of the furniture had been overthrown by the crash. The pictures on the starboard side were clinging to the walls, while those on the port side were hanging at least a foot away. The submarine had a marked list to starboard, and was perfectly still.

There came the sound of voices and hasty steps. Ned and Terray entered the saloon.

" What's happened?" the Professor asked.

" That's what we've come to ask you, sir," replied Terray.

" It's easy enough to figure it out for yourself," said the Canadian grimly. " The *Nautilus* has struck—and judging by the way she's lying right now, I guess it's not going to be easy to right her again."

" Very true, Mr. Land," said a voice behind him. " The situation is, without doubt, a serious one."

The three swung round. Captain Nemo had entered the saloon. His face was very grave.

" So the *Nautilus* has stranded?" the Professor asked.

" Yes."

" What happened, Captain?"

" Something quite unforeseen. An enormous block of ice has broken from a berg, and turned right over in the water. It struck the *Nautilus* as it fell, and then, gliding under its hull, raised it again as it swung back. My vessel is now lying on its side on a shelf of this ice-block—with the iceberg itself above. And this at a depth of a hundred and eighty fathoms."

There was a little silence while the three men thought over this startling news.

" Can't we get off by emptying the reservoirs?" asked Terray. " She should right herself if you do that."

" That is being done at this moment. You can hear the pumps working. My instruments show that the *Nautilus* is rising, but the block of ice is rising with it. Until something stops its upward movement, we can do little to better our position."

A terrible thought entered the Professor's mind. No doubt the *Nautilus* would right itself when the block stopped rising; but at any moment the submarine might strike the bottom of the berg and be crushed between the two glassy surfaces. . . .

Suddenly a slight movement was felt through the vessel. It seemed to be righting itself a little. Things hanging in the saloon were returned to their normal position. The cabin walls seemed more upright. No one spoke. With beating hearts they watched and felt the straightening. Two or three minutes passed.

" She's righted herself," said Terray, excitedly.

" Yes," Captain Nemo agreed, and he pointed to the port and starboard observation-ports in turn. " The block has stopped rising—but we have not yet escaped."

Through the ports, on either side, and at a distance of about ten yards, rose dazzling walls of ice. The *Nautilus* was still rising; the ice-walls were moving slowly by. . . .

There came another slight shock, and the submarine was suddenly motionless. In that moment, they all guessed what had happened. The submarine had struck the lower surface of the iceberg, which stretched over her like an immense ceiling. The ice-block had found a resting-place on the upright walls, lodging itself so that the *Nautilus* was trapped—imprisoned in a kind of tunnel, filled with quiet water. The only way she could move was

either forward or backward—moving under
the iceberg until she reached the end of it.
Here, at least, there still remained a chance
of escape.

Captain Nemo hurried from the saloon. A
few seconds later the submarine began to move
slowly along the tunnel. The Professor and his
friends stood silently beside a port. The
searchlights were brilliantly reflected by the
walls of ice on either hand, and above. Every
angle, every little ridge of ice, threw back a
dazzling reflection.

A moment or two later there came another
shock at the bows of the submarine. The three
men were thrown across the cabin.

" She's stuck!" gasped Ned.

" Perhaps Captain Nemo will find a way out,"
said the Professor quietly.

They picked themselves up and stared through
the port once more.

" He's moving backwards," said Professor
Arronax. " This end of the tunnel must be
blocked. He'll have to try the other end."

He tried to make himself sound as if he were
quite sure that there *would* be a way out. The
backward speed of the submarine increased. The
ice-walls flashed by. The minutes passed. Then
came another shock, that shuddered all through
the hull. The three looked at each other

without a word. A moment later Captain Nemo entered the saloon.

" Gentlemen," he said quietly, " the iceberg has shifted and closed every outlet. The *Nautilus* is trapped."

CHAPTER TEN

Want of Air

THE awful truth sank home. All round the *Nautilus* were solid walls of ice. They were prisoners in these frozen depths.

Captain Nemo's face was very grave.

"There are two ways of dying in these circumstances," he said. "The first is to be crushed; the second is to die of suffocation. Let us then calculate our chances."

"How long can we expect the air-supply to last?" the Professor asked.

Captain Nemo shrugged.

"Four to five days—if we are careful," he said.

"Is there any chance of our escaping in that time?"

"There is a chance that we could do so by piercing one of the walls that surround us."

"On which side?"

"Sound will tell us which is the least thick. I am going to ground the *Nautilus* on the lower bank, and my men will attack the ice on the thinnest side."

Captain Nemo went out. Soon there came a hissing noise as water entered the submarine's reservoirs. She sank slowly, and at last came to rest on the lower bank at a depth of just over one thousand feet.

" My friends," said the Professor, " our safety is in our own hands. We cannot stand idle while others work."

" Guess you're right," agreed Ned. " C'mon, let's lend a hand."

They found Captain Nemo in the act of putting on a diving-suit, along with other members of his crew. He gladly accepted their offer of help.

" There are many hours of hard work before us," he said, " so we must take it in turns to work and rest. Mr. Land, I should be glad if you would join my working-party, and the Professor and Mr. Terray join the party that will take over in two hours' time."

The Canadian began putting on a diving-suit, and was ready as soon as the others.

The Professor and his assistant went back to the saloon and posted themselves beside a port. Some moments later, they saw a dozen of the crew set foot on the ice-bank. Ned and Captain Nemo were with them.

Before attacking the walls, Captain Nemo took soundings, to be sure of working in the

right direction. Long metal rods were sunk in
the side walls, which were found to be far too
thick for any attempt to be made on them. It
was useless to attack the ceiling, so Captain
Nemo then sounded the lower surface. There,
he discovered, about ten yards of ice separated
the submarine from the water.

It seemed clear enough that they must try to
cut a way downwards.

The Captain set his men to mark out a trench,
rather larger than the submarine's hull, and
about eight yards to one side of it. The men set
to work with their pickaxes, and were soon
shifting quite large blocks of ice.

After two hours' hard work, the trench-
digging party came in exhausted. The Professor
and Terray went out with a new party of
workers. The water seemed cold at first, but
they soon grew warm handling the pickaxes.
The Professor found that his movements were
free enough, although they were made under a
pressure of thirty atmospheres.

When he came back inside, two hours later,
the atmosphere of the *Nautilus* seemed very
heavy after the pure air-supply of his diving-
suit.

The work went on, in two-hour shifts, all
through that day and night. But next morning
the Professor became aware of a new danger.

The side walls were gradually closing in, as the beds of water farthest from the submarine slowly froze solid. If this went on, the walls of ice would close in on the submarine with a pressure strong enough to burst its steel hull as if it were only glass.

When he went inside again he told Captain Nemo of his fears.

" I know it," said Nemo calmly, " but I can see no way of stopping it. The only chance is for us to work more quickly than the walls can close in."

By evening they had managed to dig a trench more than seven feet deep. The next morning they were down to sixteen feet, but the side walls were thickening visibly. The wall to port had advanced to at least four yards from the hull of the *Nautilus*.

For an instant, the Professor was filled with despair. What was the good of digging if he must be suffocated in the end, crushed by the water that was turning into stone?

Just then Captain Nemo passed near him. The Professor touched his hand and showed him the walls of their prison. The Captain understood and signed for the Professor to follow him. They went on board and removed their diving-helmets.

" Professor," said Nemo gravely, " we must

" Man to Beast ?" he said. " Fight those things ?" (Page 85)

find some way of stopping the walls freezing, or we shall be crushed in a matter of hours.''

'' What can we do?'' asked the Professor. '' The water is freezing on every side. How long will the air-supply last?''

The Captain looked him straight in the face.

'' Until tomorrow evening,'' he said.

A cold sweat broke over the Professor's body. In that moment, his lungs seemed to be without air already.

Then Captain Nemo smacked one fist hard into the palm of the other hand.

'' Boiling water,'' he muttered.

The Professor stared.

'' Boiling water?'' he cried.

'' Yes. We are shut in a very little space. If we pumped out jets of boiling water wouldn't they raise the temperature in this part and halt the freezing?''

The Professor gave a cry.

'' Almost certainly,'' he said. '' Let's try it.''

He followed Captain Nemo to the galleys, where there stood the machines that supplied drinking water by evaporation. They filled these with water and turned on the heat. When the water was boiling, they called in the working-party, and began pumping out the heated water. They kept this up for several hours. When they started, the thermometer had stood

6 (H 204)

at seven degrees below zero outside. Four hours later it had risen to four degrees.

The pumps were kept going all night. In the morning the temperature had risen to one degree below zero, and work began once more upon the trench. Over ten feet of ice remained to be cleared. That, according to Captain Nemo, would take something close on forty-eight hours. The air could not be renewed inside the *Nautilus*, and the coming day would make matters worse.

That afternoon, when the Professor came inside to rest, a great weight seemed to hang upon him. Huge yawns almost dislocated his jaws. His lungs panted and felt as if they were burning. He lay back, feeling powerless, almost unconscious.

He was glad to go back outside when his turn came round again, even though his arms ached terribly and the skin had been torn off his hands. What did his tiredness matter so long as he was breathing the pure air that was supplied by the apparatus on his diving-suit?

By the end of that day only five feet of ice separated the submarine from the open sea. The air-supply inside the vessel was becoming really foul now. Next morning the Professor had pains in his head, and a dizziness that made him reel like a drunken man. The others were the same. Some of the crew had rattling in the throat.

That morning Captain Nemo decided that the time had come for a last, desperate effort to crush the ice-bed that separated them from the sea.

He gave orders that the reservoirs were to be emptied. The *Nautilus* began to float, and the crew towed it so as to bring it over the trench. Then, partly filling his reservoirs again, Captain Nemo lowered the submarine directly into the hole.

Everyone came on board. The hatches were screwed down, and the *Nautilus* then rested on a bed of ice which was only a few feet thick, and which had been pierced by the sounding rods in a hundred different places. The taps of the reservoirs were opened and the water was let in, increasing the weight of the submarine to eighteen thousand tons.

Every man on board waited and listened in a breathless silence. Their lives depended on the next few minutes.

All at once came a humming sound from the hull of the *Nautilus*. The ice cracked with a strange noise like tearing paper—and the submarine sank.

" We're away," croaked Terray.

The Professor couldn't even answer him. His

head was swimming and he was gasping and panting for breath.

The *Nautilus* sank like a stone under the frightful weight it was carrying. The pumps were switched on to empty the reservoirs in part. The fall was stopped. The submarine rose a little; the motors raced; the screw, turning at full speed, made the hull tremble to its very bolts. The *Nautilus*—filled with foul air and with every man on board gasping for breath—drove on beneath the iceberg.

The Professor lay stretched out on the floor of the saloon. His face was purple, his lips blue. He felt as if he were going to die. The *Nautilus* was moving at a frightful pace, tearing through the water at forty miles an hour.

Where was Captain Nemo?

At that moment he was at the helm, his face calm, his eyes fixed on the instruments before him. The submarine had shot out from beneath the iceberg. They were only twenty feet below the surface. A mere plate of ice separated them from the atmosphere. Could they break through it? Captain Nemo was going to make the attempt.

The submarine's nose came up. It drove at the ice-field from beneath, like a huge battering-ram. The ice gave way. The submarine shot forward on to the icy plain above, which cracked apart and was crushed beneath its weight.

Men rushed to tear open the hatches. At last a stream of pure, life-giving air flowed into all parts of the submarine.

CHAPTER ELEVEN

New Enemies

THE Professor had no idea how he had got up to the platform. He learned later that Ned Land had carried him there. He lay back on the iron hull, drawing the icy air into his lungs.

He felt his strength returning. He raised his head and looked round the ice-field, feeling the breeze upon his cheeks. Ned Land put a hand upon his shoulder.

" After that little episode," he said grimly, " I've no further doubts about Captain Nemo. Who but a madman would have tried to sail beneath the South Pole?"

" The fact remains that he succeeded in doing it," said the Professor.

" The fact remains that we don't know what crazy notion he'll be wanting to try next," said Ned impatiently. " Where do we go from here? Will he take us into the Pacific or the Atlantic? When shall we get another chance to make a break for it?"

The Professor had no idea. He feared in his

heart that Captain Nemo would turn back towards the Pacific, towards those vast waters in
which the *Nautilus* could sail freely. At all
events, it should not be long before they knew
which way they were going.

A few hours later the *Nautilus* was pursuing
her course to the north, her oxygen supplies re-
plenished, and her crew seeming to have
forgotten their sufferings under the ice.

The submarine went on at a rapid pace. The
polar circle was left behind, and the course
shaped for Cape Horn.

Captain Nemo did not appear in the saloon.
A week passed, then a second week. Water
glided by the observation-ports, while the days
glided into nights, and the nights into days. The
Professor and his friends ate, slept, woke up,
and watched the water gliding past once more.
Steadily there grew in them a new hope—the
hope that they might make their escape—for
Captain Nemo had taken the *Nautilus* back into
the Atlantic, and was following the American
coastline.

The submarine travelled north across the
mouth of the Amazon; the equator was crossed.
Each day the Professor studied the planisphere
on which the course was marked.

Then, for several days, the *Nautilus* veered
away from the American coast. There came a

day when she surfaced and the Professor sighted Guadaloupe at a distance of thirty miles.

The three captives held a long talk on their chances of making an escape. For six months now they had been prisoners on board the *Nautilus*; and, as Ned Land said, it was high time their captivity was brought to an end.

Since their Antarctic adventure, Captain Nemo had seemed to shun the three. They saw him rarely, and he no longer came to the saloon. What change had come over him, they wondered. For what cause? They had no answer, except Ned's suggestion: "He's getting crazier than ever."

The Professor had come round to Ned's way of thinking. He could now write the true book of underwater life; and this book, sooner or later, he wanted to offer to the world at large.

He was still making notes. Each day, in the seas off the Leeward Islands, what interesting creatures he saw through the ports!

When they were off the Bahamas, the submarine was floating among high underwater cliffs, all covered with large weeds and plants.

"These are the breeding-grounds of the giant octopus," the Professor remarked to Terray. "In these depths I believe they grow to an immense size."

"Now, that's a creature I've never run

across,'' said Ned. '' I've fished in the wrong waters, I guess. How big can they get?''

'' There are some skeletons in the museums of Trieste and Montpelier that are more than six feet across,'' the Professor answered, '' but you must remember that a creature so big would have tentacles twenty-seven feet long. There have been others reported even larger than that.''

For a second or two Ned had been shifting uneasily on his seat, his eyes glued on one of the observation-ports.

'' Well,'' he drawled slowly, '' if you take a peek through that port, I guess you might see the great-grandfather of one of those skeletons.''

The Professor and Terray swung round. Both gasped and wrinkled their noses in disgust. Before their eyes, just beyond the port, was a horrible monster. It was an immense octopus, about eight feet long. It was swimming in the same direction as the Nautilus, and watching the men with its huge, staring eyes. Its eight arms, which were fixed to its head, were twice as long as its body. Its mouth was a horned beak, like a parrot's.

'' What a horrible beast!'' exclaimed Ned.

A moment later more of the creatures appeared. They formed a procession after the Nautilus, and the Professor could hear their beaks gnashing against the hull. He took up a pencil and began to sketch the nearest creature.

Then, of a sudden, the *Nautilus* came to a shuddering halt. A shock made it tremble in every plate.

" Have we struck something?" asked Terray.

" I guess so," said the Canadian, " but it can't be too bad, for we're still floating."

Captain Nemo entered the saloon. He said nothing, but went to an observation-port and peered at the hideous creatures outside.

" We've picked up a fine collection of followers," said the Professor.

Captain Nemo nodded.

" Yes," he said, " and I'm afraid we shall have to fight them, man to beast."

The Professor stared up at him, wondering if he had heard aright.

" Man to beast?" he said. " Fight those things?"

" Yes. The screw has stopped turning. I believe that the horny jaws of one of those monsters are entangled in the blades."

" What are you planning to do?"

" Rise to the surface, and drive off the creatures. We shall have to attack them with hatchets. My electric bullets would be of little use against their soft flesh, where they wouldn't meet enough resistance to go off."

Ned Land rose to his feet.

" I'd like to join you, Captain," he said. " This is my line of work, only I'd rather use a harpoon than a hatchet."

" Glad to have you, Mr. Land," said the Captain. " Follow me."

The three men followed Captain Nemo to the central staircase. About ten of the crew, all armed with hatchets, were waiting there, ready for the attack. Terray and the Professor took two hatchets; a harpoon was found for Ned. By that time the *Nautilus* had risen to the surface. A sailor began unfastening the hatch of the conning-tower.

The bolts were hardly loosened when the hatch rose suddenly, drawn back by the suckers of an octopus's arm. Immediately, one of these arms slid like a serpent through the opening. Captain Nemo sprang up the stairs and severed this tentacle with one blow of his axe. It slid wriggling down the ladder. The whole party pressed forward up the stairs and out on to the platform.

As the Professor stepped out, he saw a sight that made his blood curdle. Two tentacles that had been lashing the air came down on a seaman who stood beside Captain Nemo and lifted him into the air. A terrible head rose out of the water alongside. The unlucky seaman gazed down at the head and screamed. Captain Nemo rushed to the side of the submarine and cut through one arm with a single blow of his axe. . . .

The Professor had no time to see more. Other monsters were creeping along the sides of the *Nautilus*. Men, everywhere, began lashing out with their axes, burying their weapons in these fleshy masses.

It was sickening work—horrible!

The Professor had one more glimpse of the unhappy seaman who was still held by an arm of the octopus, which brandished its victim in the air as if he were a feather. As Captain Nemo attacked once more, the animal shot out a stream of black liquid and sank from sight, taking the screaming man with it. His cries were suddenly cut short.

There were at least a dozen of the creatures all round the submarine. The men were bawling in a kind of frenzy of rage. At every stroke, Ned Land's harpoon was plunged into the staring eyes of an octopus—until, in an instant, he was seized and overthrown by the tentacles of a monster that came behind. . . .

The Professor called out in horror, and rushed towards his friend, but Captain Nemo was there ahead of him. His axe flashed once in the sunlight, then disappeared between the two enormous jaws of the octopus. Ned Land struggled to his feet and plunged his harpoon deep in the creature's flesh. The monster sank back, releasing its hold on Ned, and squirting ink as it went.

The struggle, which had lasted a quarter of an hour, was over. One by one, the monsters, beaten and mutilated, sank beneath the waves. The men were left, panting hard, upon the little deck. Captain Nemo stood for a moment looking into the sea that had swallowed up one of his crew, then turned and went below without another word.

CHAPTER TWELVE

The Avenger

*T was many days before the memory of that awful struggle faded from the Professor's mind. During those days he saw nothing of Captain Nemo, who had taken the *Nautilus* out into the Atlantic, as if he were setting course for Europe.

Again, the three captives began to discuss their chances of escape. Ned was all for stealing the boat at once, and hoping that they would be picked up by a transatlantic steamer. Only one thing held him back for the moment. That was the weather, which was very bad, so that even he was forced to agree that it would be suicide to tempt the sea in a little, open boat.

His temper grew more and more ragged. He found it hard to bear the long imprisonment. He wanted to be free and doing things in the world of men. Even the Professor was seized with longing for his old life. Nearly seven months had passed without their hearing any news from land.

The weather continued bad; the *Nautilus*

continued her course across the Atlantic. There came an evening when she was no more than a hundred and twenty miles from the coast of Ireland.

Next day, when the submarine surfaced at noon, the sea was quiet and the sky clear. The Professor went up to the platform and found Captain Nemo already there, taking his bearings. The Professor stood quietly, looking round upon the sea while he drank in the fresh air.

Then he gave a great start!

About four miles to the east he could see a large steam vessel. The ship was too far away for him to judge its nationality, but it seemed to be making straight for the submarine.

Captain Nemo gave no sign that he had seen the ship. He was busy sighting the sun, his sextant to his eye. The *Nautilus* was motionless.

An instant later a dull booming sound came drifting over the water. The Professor looked at the Captain. Nemo did not turn or move.

" Captain Nemo!" said the Professor sharply.

There was no answer. Feet clattered on the metal treads of the stair. Ned Land and Terray swung themselves on to the platform. Captain Nemo did not even turn his head.

The Professor pointed to the oncoming ship. Ned Land gave a cry, and his eyes blazed with excitement.

" I heard a gunshot," he said.

At that moment Captain Nemo lowered his sextant and went below, without a glance at the three on the platform.

All three stared towards the ship. It seemed to be putting on steam.

" What is she?" asked the Professor.

" A warship," answered Ned. " I can tell by her masts and rigging. With any luck," he added grimly, " she may sink this cursed *Nautilus*."

" I doubt it," said Terray slowly. " She can't attack beneath the waves."

The Canadian screwed up his eyes, and peered towards the ship.

" She's showing no colours," he said, " but she's a warship, all right."

They stood there, watching the ship approach. A thick, black smoke was pouring from her funnels. Before long, they could see a pennant floating like a thin ribbon from her mainmast.

" If she comes much closer," said Ned, " then I'm going over the side. If we swim towards her, she's bound to stop and pick us up."

The Professor nodded, his eyes fixed on the oncoming ship. Whether English, French, Russian, or American, she would be sure to take them in—if only they could reach her.

Suddenly a puff of white smoke broke upon

the warship's bows, followed by the boom of a gun. A jet of water struck up close to the nose of the submarine. Its spray spattered on the hull.

" They're firing at us," said the Professor, startled and amazed. " Surely they can see that there are men on board?"

It was the last thing he had expected to happen.

" I guess the *Abraham Lincoln* got back to port," said Ned. " The whole world must know, by now, that the " monster " is a sub-marine—something much more dangerous than any creature of the seas."

A whole flood of light burst upon the Pro-fessor's mind. Ned was right of, course. It was likely that there were warships on every ocean, seeking this new and terrible instrument of destruction. The world had learned that Cap-tain Nemo used his submarine for some unknown vengeance of his own. The nations must have united against this man who had vowed a deadly hatred for them. Instead of meeting friends on board the approaching ship, the Professor and his companions could expect only pitiless enemies.

A third shot came from the ship with a vicious hum. Another jet of water was struck up close by the submarine. The warship was no more than two miles off.

Ned clutched the Professor's arm.

" I guess it's time we got ourselves out of this mess," he said. " Let's signal to them. Maybe they'll realise there are *some* honest folk aboard."

He tugged a handkerchief from his pocket and began waving it above his head—but only for a second. Someone moved swiftly across the platform from behind; something crashed down upon his head; he crumpled up on the deck.

Terray and the Professor swung round. Behind them stood Captain Nemo, the pistol with which he had clubbed Ned down now gripped in his fist, its muzzle pointed straight at them.

" You fools!" snarled Captain Nemo. " Do you wish me to destroy *you* before I deal with this ship?"

For a second he looked away across the water, towards the approaching vessel, and in his eyes was the light of a terrible hatred. His face was deadly pale. Another shot sailed overhead. Captain Nemo showed his teeth in a mirthless grin.

" Fire away!" he cried. " Fire away, while you can. In a very little while I'll send you to the bottom of the sea."

Gone was the ice-cool Captain Nemo they had known in the past. He was like a madman. Terray and the Professor gaped at him in utter astonishment. At their feet, Ned Land sat up groaning, one hand on his head.

Captain Nemo waved his pistol.

" Go below," he said harshly, " and take the Canadian with you."

" Captain," said the Professor urgently, " you can't mean to sink this ship?"

Captain Nemo's eyes blazed.

" The attack is about to begin," he said. " Now, go below!"

" What is this vessel?" the Professor persisted.

" You don't know? So much the better! Its nationality to you, at least, will remain a secret. Go down!"

There was no choice for it. Between them, the Professor and Terray helped the dazed Canadian to his feet. His legs seemed like rubber and he stumbled as he walked, but they managed to get him down the stairs. As they went, a shot whined overhead.

There was a shout of fury from Captain Nemo. As they moved along the passage to the saloon, they heard the hatch of the conning-tower slammed home.

They reached the saloon. Ned sank down on to a seat, his head in his hands, then looked up with a wry grin.

" I asked for that, I guess," he said.

" You did, Mr. Land," said a cold voice.

Captain Nemo stood in the doorway.

" You must understand," he went on, " that whoever enters the *Nautilus* will never be allowed to leave it again, to reveal its secrets. You are here to stay."

" Captain Nemo," said the Professor quietly, " you can't mean to sink that ship—to kill hundreds of men——"

" I do, and I shall," broke in Captain Nemo, eyes blazing with anger. " Here, I am the law and the judge. I have passed sentence on those men, as once their accursed nation passed sentence on me. I was imprisoned for years, because I would not reveal secrets that I thought it better the nations should not have—the secret of the power that drives my *Nautilus*— the secrets of her construction. Through my own countrymen I lost all that I loved—wife, children, father and mother. All that I hate is out there, on board that ship. It shall be sunk. Say no more!"

He turned on his heel and left the saloon. Two minutes later the *Nautilus* dived, her hull vibrating as she raced through the water.

Without a word, their faces grey, the three men in the saloon turned to an observation-port. They understood only too well what was about to happen. It was too late to act. The *Nautilus* did not mean to fight on the surface, but would strike at the warship below the waterline.

The Professor and his companions would have to be unwilling witnesses of the dreadful drama that was approaching. They had scarcely time to think about it. They looked at each other without speaking. A kind of numbness had taken hold of the Professor's mind. Thought seemed to stand still. He just waited and listened, every sense merged in that of hearing.

The *Nautilus* was tearing through the water. The whole vessel trembled with her speed.

Suddenly all three men cried out together. . . .

The shock as the submarine's nose struck the hull of the warship was surprisingly slight. The Professor could *feel*, however, all through his body, the penetrating power of the submarine. He heard metallic rattling and tearing and scrapings. The *Nautilus*, driven on by its fantastic speed, passed through the hull of the warship like a needle through sailcloth.

All three of the watchers in the saloon had a glimpse of the dark mass through which the *Nautilus* drove. That was all. But their imaginations could picture the terrible scene above. . . .

The warship, with the great hole torn in her side, would heave and lurch, while the water thundered in below her decks. Men—shouting, screaming, panic-stricken—would be rushing everywhere; some would cling to the masts, others would be hurled into the water. . . .

The *Nautilus* sped on beneath the waves. Suddenly, behind her, there was a loud explosion, as if the magazines of the warship had caught fire.

The submarine began to turn, slowed, and moved back the way she had come. A minute later Ned Land gave a ghastly cry. His gaze was glued to the observation-port. He raised a trembling hand and pointed.

Through the green swirl of the water a large mass was slowly sinking. It was the battered, broken hull of the ship. There were men still struggling under the water to release her life-boats. It was like watching an ant-heap overtaken by a flood.

The Professor was filled with horror. His hair stood on end. He was sickened and disgusted by the terrible thing that Captain Nemo had done.

Down and down sank the stricken ship. Her topmast, laden with victims, appeared; then her spars, bending under the weight of men; and last of all the top of her mainmast. Then the dark mass disappeared, and with it the crew. . .

Captain Nemo had taken his revenge.

CHAPTER THIRTEEN

The Whirlpool

IT was night. At wonderful speed, a hundred feet beneath the waves, the *Nautilus* raced on its way.

Professor Arronax lay sleepless upon his bunk. He found it hard to sleep, for he was troubled by dreadful nightmares.

He hardly knew how many days had passed since the sinking of the warship. It must have been nine or ten, he guessed. In all that time, he had seen nothing of Captain Nemo. He no longer wished to see him. The very thought of the man filled him with horror. Whatever the Captain might have suffered in the past, he had no right to punish in the terrible way he had chosen.

What mad plan had he now in mind? Where was the submarine going? Where was the man flying, after his dreadful act of war against humanity?

The Professor did not know. For the past week no course had been marked upon the planisphere in the saloon. The submarine had kept under water as much as possible, surfacing only for short periods to renew the supply of air. The Professor guessed, though he knew that he could well be mistaken, that the *Nautilus* was hurrying towards the northern seas.

Towards the early hours of that morning, he fell into a restless sleep. He was awakened by a touch upon the face. He started. A dark shape was leaning over him. A voice spoke, softly.

" It's all right, Professor. It's me—Ned Land."

The Professor sat up.

" What is it?" he whispered.

" We're going to escape," said Ned. " We've got it all worked out, Terray and I."

The Professor showed no sign of surprise.

" When?" he asked. " At dawn?"

" No," said Ned, " we'll have to wait for darkness. I'm telling you now, so that there'll be no chance of our being overheard in the saloon. This is the plan. Just before ten o'clock tonight, I'm going to get into the pilot's cabin, and put the helmsman to sleep. You know what I mean. I got Captain Nemo to tell me something about the controls a while back, and I reckon I can bring the *Nautilus* to the surface. Then we'll make a break for it in the boat. If the job's done quietly, no one need know. I want you to be at the bottom of the central staircase at ten tonight."

" I'll be there. Do you know where we are?"

" We were in sight of land yesterday, but I don't know what country. It doesn't really matter, anyway. The sea's bad, and the wind's high, but I think we can manage in the boat. I've got hold of some food and some bottles of water. We'll just have to chance it."

" All right, Ned. I'll be ready."

The Canadian stole out again. The Professor lay back and waited for the coming of dawn. As it happened, the *Nautilus* was brought to the surface at first light. The Professor went up to the platform then, making his way there with difficulty. The submarine was rocking to the beat of the waves. The morning was cold and grey, the sky threatening, but, far off, the Professor thought that he could see the shadowy outline of a coast.

How long that day seemed—the last he would spend on board the submarine, if all went well. Ned and Terray said little, as they sat in the saloon, for fear of betraying themselves. They dined at six that evening, forcing themselves to eat, though none of them was hungry. A little after eight, the Professor went to his cabin and lay upon his bunk. Ned Land came to him an hour later.

" I shan't see you again till we're ready to go," he said. " Get to the bottom of the staircase a minute before ten."

The Canadian stole out again, without waiting for an answer. Half an hour later, the Professor rose and put on some strong sea-clothing. He collected all his notes and sketches and stowed them about his person. His heart was beating loudly. He still had a quarter of an hour to wait.

Where was Captain Nemo, he wondered? What was he doing at this moment?

The time passed very slowly. He listened with every sense for some sound to tell him what was going on aboard the submarine. Where was Ned? Had he succeeded in his plan of putting the helmsman to sleep? Was it his imagination, or was the submarine rising. . . .

He looked at his watch. It was time for him to join his two companions.

He opened his door carefully. He crept along the dark passages of the *Nautilus*, stopping at each step to calm the beating of his heart. He was almost at the central staircase. A shadow was lurking at its foot.

" Professor?" whispered a voice. It was that of Terray.

The two waited in silence. There was no sound. A third figure glided towards them.

" She's on the surface," whispered Ned.
" Come on, we've no time to lose."

He went up the stairs as quietly as a cat. The
others crept after him. There came a slight
grating noise. The hatch swung open. Above
his head the Professor saw a patch of starlit sky.
A cold breeze blew on his cheeks. A moment
later, he was out on the platform. Ned Land
grabbed him by the shoulder, and swung him
towards the boat.

Ned and Terray crouched down beside the
after tower, working at the bolts which held the
boat to the submarine. Wind whipped the Professor's hair about his face. He stared round at
the angry sea. . . .

Angry sea? No, it was more than that. There
was a *pace*, a movement, about it that was un-
canny—and what was that awful roaring sound?

A terrible suspicion entered his mind. Could
the *Nautilus* be off the dangerous coast of
Norway? Was it possible that Ned had brought
her to the surface at a point somewhere between
the islands of Ferroe and Loffoden? A point
where the pent-up waters, at flood tide, rush
together with irresistible violence to form a
whirlpool from which no ship ever escapes?
Was the *Nautilus* being drawn into this gulf at
the very moment the boat was going to be
launched from its side?

Bracing himself against the raging wind, the Professor stared all round. From every point of the horizon enormous waves were meeting. The submarine was describing a wide circle on the surface of the sea. It was being carried along at a giddy speed. The Professor felt dizzy.

Suddenly a voice was heard inside the submarine. Other voices took up the cry.

The Professor was filled with dread. What noise there was around the submarine! What roarings echoed miles away!

The boat was almost free. Ned Land slid it along its grooves, grabbed the Professor's arm and shoved him into it.

The hull of the submarine began to make alarming cracking sounds. It rocked frightfully, then almost stood upright. Ned Land looked around, realising, at last, the awfulness of their situation.

" We must hold on," he cried above the wind, " and look after the bolts. We may still be saved if we stick to the *Nautilus*——"

He had not finished the words when there came a crashing noise. The bolts gave way, and the boat, torn from its grooves, was hurled like a stone from a sling into the midst of the whirlpool.

The Professor's head struck on a piece of iron. There was an instant of pain, and then everything went dark.

CHAPTER FOURTEEN

The End of Captain Nemo

SLOWLY the world came back. The Professor opened his eyes. Voices became faces and wavering, shadowy shapes became bodies. Ned Land and Terray were bending over him. Other men stood behind them, and there was a low roof overhead.

Ned Land grinned down at him.

" Well, we made it, Professor," he drawled, " though I guess we were pretty lucky."

The Professor put a hand to his head.

" Where are we?" he asked. " What happened to the *Nautilus*?"

" You're in a fisherman's cottage, on the Loffoden Isles," Ned told him. " We got washed ashore, and these people picked us up. Don't ask me how the boat lived in that sea, Professor. It was nothing short of a miracle. We must have been right on the edge of the whirl-pool to start with, and then we got tossed about all over the place for I don't know how long. The boat was overturned before we got to this

shore—you were out for the count, and we had
to drag you through the water. Anyway, we
made it—though I wouldn't like to say the same
for the *Nautilus*. I just don't know what
happened to Captain Nemo and his men. Maybe
they pulled out of it, and maybe they didn't.
It's hard to believe they were as lucky as we
were. . . ."

Remembering those last terrible seconds on
board the submarine, the Professor also found
it hard to believe that the *Nautilus* had escaped
from the whirlpool. Even now, perhaps, she
lay broken on the sharp rocks at the bottom of
those dangerous waters, the bodies of her commander and crew strewn all around.

And yet, there was always the chance that the
submarine had escaped. . . .

During the next few weeks the Professor had
plenty of time to speculate upon the fate of
Captain Nemo and the first submarine vessel the
world had ever known. The means of com-
munication between the north of Norway and
the south were, seemingly, very rare. The
three who had escaped from the submarine had
to wait for the steamboat running monthly from
Cape North.

The Professor began to write down all the
strange adventures they had gone through since
Captain Nemo had taken them on board the

Nautilus. Not a fact was left out, not a detail exaggerated. It was the true story of their incredible expedition beneath the waters, where man had never voyaged before.

Long before he had finished, he began to wonder if he would be believed. He did not know. And it mattered very little, after all. What he did know was that he had a right to speak of those seas under which, in seven months, he had crossed twenty thousand leagues, in that submarine tour of the world which had revealed so many wonders.

All the time, at the back of his mind, there remained one question: what had become of the *Nautilus*? Did it escape from the whirlpool? Was Captain Nemo still alive? If so, would he continue to make war upon the shipping he met on the open seas?

He also wondered if he would ever know the true name of the man who had devised such a wonderful vessel as the *Nautilus*; or if the nationality of the warship that had been sunk would give a clue to the nationality of Captain Nemo.

The Professor hoped so. He also hoped that the *Nautilus* had conquered the sea at that terrible gulf. If that were so—if Captain Nemo still lived beneath the waters, he hoped that the hatred in his heart would now be quietened.

Right at the end of his account of his adventures on board the *Nautilus* the Professor wrote these words:

" I trust that Captain Nemo still lives, and has found some measure of peace in that wonderful world in which he lives and moves. If he still lives in the ocean, his adopted country, may he find peace in contemplating the wonders that are revealed to him. May his love for these things fill all his being, so that the spirit of vengeance is for ever extinguished!

" Let it be remembered, in the spirit of forgiveness, that Captain Nemo was the first being to venture into the depths of the mighty seas. . . ."